John Giles

Memoirs of odd adventures, strange deliverances, etc. in the captivity of John Giles

SALZWASSER
VERLAG

John Giles

Memoirs of odd adventures, strange deliverances, etc. in the captivity of John Giles

1st Edition | ISBN: 978-3-75250-444-6

Place of Publication: Frankfurt am Main, Germany

Year of Publication: 2020

Salzwasser Verlag GmbH, Germany.

Reprint of the original, first published in 1869.

MEMOIRS

OF

ODD ADVENTURES,

STRANGE DELIVERANCES, ETC.

IN THE

CAPTIVITY OF JOHN GILES, ESQ.,

COMMANDER OF THE GARRISON ON SAINT GEORGE RIVER, IN THE
DISTRICT OF MAINE.

WRITTEN BY HIMSELF.

ORIGINALLY PUBLISHED AT BOSTON, 1736.

PRINTED FOR WILLIAM DODGE.

CINCINNATI:
SPILLER & GATES, PRINTERS, 168 VINE STREET.
1869.

INTRODUCTION.

THESE private memoirs were collected from my minutes, at the earnest request of my second consort, for the use of our family, that we might have a memento ever ready at hand, to excite in ourselves gratitude and thankfulness to God; and in our offspring a due sense of their dependence on the Sovereign of the universe, from the precariousness and vicissitudes of all sublunary enjoyments. In this state, and for this end, they have laid by me for some years. They at length falling into the hands of some, for whose judgment I had a value, I was pressed for a copy for the public. Others, desiring of me to extract particulars from them, which the multiplicity and urgency of my affairs would not admit, I have now determined to suffer their publication. I have not made scarce any addition to this manual, except in the chapter of *creatures*, which I was urged to make larger. I might have greatly enlarged it, but I feared it would grow beyond its proportion. I have been likewise advised to give a particular account of my father, which I am not very fond of, having no dependence on the virtues or honors of my ancestors to recommend me to the favor of God or men ; nevertheless, because some think it is a respect due to the memory of my parents, whose name I was obliged to mention in the following story, and a satisfaction which their posterity might justly expect from me, I shall give some account of him, though as brief as possible.

The flourishing state of New England, before the unhappy eastern wars, drew my father hither, whose first settlement was on Kennebeck river, at a place called Merrymeeting Bay, where he dwelt for some years; until, on the death of my grand parents, he, with his family returned to England, to settle his affairs. This done, he came over with the design to have returned to his farm ; but on his arrival at Boston, the eastern Indians had begun their hostilities. He therefore begun a settlement on Long Island. The air of that place not so well agreeing with his constitution, and the Indians having become peaceable, he again proposed to resettle his lands in Merrymeeting Bay ; but finding that place deserted, and that plantations were going on at Pemmaquid, he purchased several tracts of land of the inhabitants there. Upon his highness the duke of York resuming a claim to those parts, my father took out patents under that claim ; and when Pemmaquid was set off by the name of the county of Cornwall, in the province of New York, he was commissioned chief justice of the same by Gov. Duncan [Dongan.]* He was a strict sabbatarian, and met with considerable difficulty in the discharge of his office, from the immoralities of a people who had long lived lawless. He laid out no inconsiderable income, which he had annually from England, on the place, and at last lost his life there, as will hereafter be related.

I am not insensible of the truth of an assertion of Sir Roger L'Estrange, that "Books and dishes have this common fate : no one of either ever pleased all tastes." And I am fully of opinion in this : "It is as little to be wished for as expected ; for a universal applause is, at least, two-thirds of a scandal." To conclude with Sir Roger, "Though I made this composition principally for my family, yet, if any man has a mind to take part with me, he has free leave, and is welcome ;" but let him carry this consideration along with him, "that he is a very unmannerly guest who forces himself upon another man's table, and then quarrels with his dinner."

---

* He had been appointed Governor of New York, 30 Sept. 1682.—S. G. DRAKE.

MEMOIRS

OF

Odd Adventures, Strange Deliverances, Etc.

CHAPTER I.

CONTAINING THE OCCURRENCES OF THE FIRST YEAR.

ON the second day of August, 1689, in the morning. my honored father, THOMAS GYLES, Esq., went with some laborers, my two elder brothers and myself, to one of his farms, which laid upon the river about three miles above fort Charles,* adjoining Pemmaquid falls, there to gather in his English harvest, and we labored securely till noon. After we had dined, our people went to their labor, some in one field to their English hay, the others to another field of English corn. My father, the youngest of my two brothers, and myself, tarried near the farm-house in which we had dined till about one of the clock, at which time we heard the report of several great guns at the fort. Upon which my father said he hoped it was a signal of good news,

---

* Fort Charles stood on the spot where fort Frederick was, not long since, founded by Colonel Dunbar. The township adjoining thereto was called Jamestown, in honor to the duke of York. In this town, within a quarter of a mile of the fort, was my father's dwelling-house, from which he went out that unhappy morning.

and that the great council had sent back the soldiers, to cover the inhabitants; (for on report of the revolution they had deserted.) But to our great surprise, about thirty or forty Indians,[*] at that moment, discharged a volley of shot at us, from behind a rising ground, near our barn. The yelling of the Indians,[†] the whistling of their shot, and the voice of my father, whom I heard cry out, "What now! what now!" so terrified me (though he seemed to be handling a gun), that I endeavored to make my escape. My brother ran one way and I another, and looking over my shoulder, I saw a stout fellow, painted, pursuing me, with a gun, and a cutlass glittering in his hand which I expected every moment in my brains. I soon fell down, and the Indian seized me by the left hand. He offered me no abuse, but tied my arms, then lifted me up and pointed to the place where the people were at work about the hay, and led me that way. As we went, we crossed where my father was, who looked very pale and bloody, and walked very slowly. When we came to the place, I saw two men shot down on the flats, and one or two more knocked on their heads with hatchets, crying out "O Lord," &c. There the Indians brought two captives, one a man, and my brother James, who, with me, had endeavored to escape by running from the house when we were first attacked. This brother was about fourteen years of

---

[*] The whole company of Indians, according to Charlevoix, was one hundred.—S. G. DRAKE.

[†] The Indians have a custom of uttering a most horrid howl when they discharge guns, designing thereby to terrify those whom they fight against.

age. My oldest brother, whose name was Thomas, wonderfully escaped by land to the Barbican, a point of land on the west side of the river, opposite the fort, where several fishing vessels lay. He got on board one of them and sailed that night.

After doing what mischief they could, they sat down and made us sit with them. After some time we arose, and the Indians pointed for us to go eastward. We marched about a quarter of a mile, and then made a halt. Here they brought my father to us. They made proposals to him, by old Moxus, who told him that those were strange Indians who shot him, and that he was sorry for it. My father replied that he was a dying man, and wanted no favor of them, but to pray with his children. This being granted him, he recommended us to the protection and blessing of God Almighty; then gave us the best advice, and took his leave for this life, hoping in God that we should meet in a better. He parted with a cheerful voice, but looked very pale, by reason of his great loss of blood, which now gushed out of his shoes. The Indians led him aside!—I heard the blows of the hatchet, but neither shriek nor groan! I afterwards heard that he had five or seven shot-holes through his waistcoat or jacket, and that he was covered with some boughs.

The Indians led us, their captives, on the east side of the river, towards the fort, and when we came within a mile and a half of the fort and town, and could see the fort, we saw fire and smoke on all sides. Here we made a short stop, and then moved within or near the distance of three-quarters of a mile from the fort, into a thick swamp. There I saw my mother and my two little sisters, and many other captives who were taken from the town. My mother asked me about my father. I told her he was killed, but could say no more for grief. She burst into tears, and the Indians moved me a little farther off, and seized me with cords to a tree.

The Indians came to New Harbor, and sent spies several days to observe how and where the people were employed, &c., who found the men were generally at work at noon, and left about their houses only women and children. Therefore the Indians divided themselves into several parties, some ambushing the way between the fort and the houses, as likewise between them and the distant fields; and then alarming the farthest off first, they killed and took the people, as they moved toward the town and fort, at their pleasure, and very few escaped to it. Mr. Pateshall was taken and killed, as he lay with his sloop near the Barbican.

On the first stir about the fort, my youngest brother was at play near it, and running in, was, by God's goodness, thus preserved. Captain Weems, with great courage and resolution, defended the weak old fort* two days; when, being much wounded, and the best of his men killed, beat for a parley, which eventuated in these conditions:

---

* I presume Charlevoix was misinformed about the strength of this place. He says: " Ils (the English) y avoient fait un fort bel establissement, défendu par un fort, qui n'étoit a la verité que de pieux, mais assez regulierement construit, avec *vingt canons montés.*"

1. That they, the Indians, should give him Mr. Pateshall's sloop.

2. That they should not molest him in carrying off the few people that had got into the fort, and three captives that they had taken.

3. That the English should carry off in their hands what they could from the fort.

On these conditions the fort was surrendered, and Captain Weems went off; and soon after, the Indians set on fire the fort and houses, which made a terrible blast, and was a melancholy sight to us poor captives, who were sad spectators.

After the Indians had thus laid waste Pemmaquid, they moved us to New Harbor, about two miles east of Pemmaquid, a cove much frequented by fishermen. At this place there were, before the war, about twelve houses. These the inhabitants deserted as soon as the rumor of war reached the place. When we turned our backs on the town, my heart was ready to break! I saw my mother. She spoke to me, but I could not answer her. That night we tarried at New Harbor, and the next day went in their canoes for Penobscot. About noon, the canoe in which my mother was, and that in which I was, came side by side; whether accidentally or by my mother's desire, I can not say. She asked me how I did. I think I said "pretty well," but my heart was so full of grief I scarcely knew whether audible to her. Then she said, "Oh! my child! how joyful and pleasant it would be if we were going to old England, to see your uncle Chalker and other friends there! Poor babe, we are going into the wilderness, the Lord knows where!' Then bursting into tears, the canoes parted. That night following, the Indians with their captives, lodged on an island.

A few days after, we arrived at Penobscot fort, where I again saw my mother, my brother and sisters, and many other captives. I think we tarried here eight days. In that time, the Jesuit of the place had a great mind to buy me. My Indian master made a visit to the Jesuit, and carried me with him. And here I will note that the Indian who takes a captive is accounted his master, and has a perfect right to him, until he gives or sells him to another. I saw the Jesuit show my master pieces of gold, and understood afterward that he was tendering them for my ransom. He gave me a biscuit, which I put into my pocket, and not daring to eat it, buried it under a log, fearing he had put something in it to make me love him. Being very young, and having heard much of the Papists torturing the Protestants, caused me to act thus; and I hated the sight of a Jesuit.* When my mother heard the talk of my being sold to a Jesuit, she said to me, "Oh! my dear child, if it were God's will, I had rather follow you to your grave, or never see you more in this world, than you should be sold to a Jesuit; for a Jesuit will ruin you, body and soul!"† It pleased

---

* It is not to be wondered at that antipathy should be so plainly exhibited at this time, considering what had been going on in England up to the latest dates; but that children should have been taught that Catholics had the power of winning over heretics by any mysterious powders, or other arts furnished them by his satanic majesty, is a matter, to say the least, of no little admiration.—S. G. DRAKE.

† It may not be improper to hear how the Jesuits themselves viewed these matters. The settlement here was, according to the French account, in their dominions, and the English settlers "incommoded extremely from thence all the Indians in the

God to grant her request, for she never saw me more! Yet she and my two little sisters were, after several years' captivity, redeemed, but she died ere I returned. My brother, who was taken with me, was, after several years' captivity, most barbarously tortured to death by the Indians.

My Indian master carried me up Penobscot river to a village called *Madawamkee*, which stands on a point of land between the main river and a branch which heads to the east of it. At home I had ever seen strangers treated with the utmost civility, and being a stranger, I expected some kind treatment here; but I soon found myself deceived, for I presently saw a number of squaws, who had got together in a circle, dancing and yelling. An old grim-looking one took me by the hand, and leading me into the ring, some seized me by the hair, and others by my hands and feet, like so many furies; but my master presently laying down a pledge, they released me.

A captive among the Indians is exposed to all manner of abuses, and to the extremest tortures, unless their master, or some of their master's relations, lay down a ransom, such as a bag of corn, a blanket, or the like, which redeems them from their cruelty for

adjacent country, who were the avowed friends of the French, and caused the government of Acadia no less inquietude, who feared, with reason, the effect of their intrigues in detaching the Indians from their alliance. The Indians, who undertook to break up the post at Pemmaquid, were Penobscots, among whom a Jesuit, named M. Thuay, a good laborer in the faith, had a numerous mission. The first attention before setting out of these brave Christians was to secure aid of the God of battles, by confessions and the sacrament; and they took care that their wives and children performed the same rites, and raised their pure hands to heaven, while their fathers and mothers went out to do battle against the heretics." See Charlevoix.—S. G. DRAKE.

that dance.   The next day we went up that eastern branch of Penobscot river many leagues; carried over land to a large pond, and from one pond to another, till, in a few days, we went down a river called Medocktack, which vents itself into St. John's river.   But before we came to the mouth of this river, we passed over a long carrying place, to Medocktack fort, which stands on a bank of St. John's river.   My master went before, and left me with an old Indian, and two or three squaws.   The old man often said (which was all the English he could speak), "By and by come to a great town and fort."   I now comforted myself in thinking how finely I should be refreshed when I came to this great town.

After some miles' travel we came in sight of a large cornfield, and soon after of the fort, to my great surprise.   Two or three squaws met us, took off my pack, and led me to a large hut or wigwam, where thirty or forty Indians were dancing and yelling round five or six poor captives, who had been taken some months before from Quochech, at the time Major Waldron was so barbarously butchered by them.   And before proceeding with my narrative, I will give a short account of that action.

Major Waldron's garrison was taken on the night of the 27th of June, 1689.*   I have heard the Indians

---

* The date stands in the old narrative, " in the beginning of April on the night after a Sabbath," which being an error, I have corrected it.   What time in the night of the 27th the place was attacked, is not mentioned, but the accounts of it are chiefly dated the day following, viz. the 28th, when the tragedy was finished.   The squaws had taken up their lodging there on the night of the 27th, and if the attack begun before midnigt, which it probably did, the date in the text is the true one.—S. G. DRAKE.

say at a feast that as there was a truce for some days, they contrived to send in two squaws to take notice of the numbers, lodgings, and other circumstances of the people in his garrison, and if they could obtain leave to lodge there, to open the gates and whistle. (They said the gates had no locks, but were fastened with pins, and that they kept no watch.) The squaws had a favorable season to prosecute their projection, for it was dull weather when they came to beg leave to lodge in the garrison. They told the major that a great many Indians were not far from thence, with a considerable quantity of beaver, who would be there to trade with him the next day. Some of the people were very much against their lodging in the garrison, but the major said, "Let the poor creatures lodge by the fire." The squaws went into every apartment, and observing the numbers in each, when all the people were asleep, arose and opened the gates, gave the signal, and the other Indians came to them; and having received an account of the state of the garrison, they divided according to the number of people in each apartment, and soon took and killed them all. The major lodged within an inner room, and when the Indians broke in upon him, he cried out: "What now! what now!" and jumping out of bed with only his shirt on, seized his sword and drove them before him through two or three doors; but for some reason, turning about toward the apartment he had just left, an Indian came up behind him, knocked him on the head with his hatchet, which stunned him, and he fell. They now seized him, dragged him out, and setting him upon a long table in his hall, bid him "judge Indians again." Then they cut and stabbed him, and he cried out "O, Lord! O, Lord!" They bid him order his book of accounts to be brought, and to cross out all the Indians' debts* (he having traded much with them). After they had tortured him to death, they burned the garrison and drew off. This narration I had from their own mouths, at a general meeting, and have reason to think it true.† But to return to my narrative.

I was whirled in among the circle of Indians, and we prisoners looked on each other with a sorrowful countenance. Presently one of them was seized by each hand and foot, by four Indians, who, swinging him up, let his back fall on the ground with full force. This they repeated till they had danced, as they called it, round the whole wigwam, which was some thirty or forty feet in length. But when they torture a boy they take him up between two. This is one of their customs of torturing captives. Another is to take up a person by the middle, with his head downward, and jolt him till one would think his bowels would shake out of his mouth. Sometimes they will take a captive by the hair of the head, and stooping him forward, strike him on the back and shoulder, till the blood gushes out of his mouth and nose. Sometimes an old shriveled squaw will take up a shovel of hot embers and throw them into a captive's bosom. If he cry

---

* When they gashed his naked breast, they said in derision, "*I cross out my account.*" —S. G. DRAKE.

† In a previous note to another narrative, I have referred the reader to my large work (The Book of the Indians), where all the circumstances of this shocking affair are detailed.—S. G. DRAKE.

out, the Indians will laugh and shout, and say, "What a brave action our old grandmother has done." Sometimes they torture them with whips, &c.

The Indians looked on me with a fierce countenance, as much as to say, it will be your turn next. They champed cornstalks, which they threw into my hat as I held it in my hand. I smiled on them, though my heart ached. I looked on one and another, but could not perceive that any eye pitied me. Presently came a squaw and a little girl, and laid down a bag of corn in the ring. The little girl took me by the hand, making signs for me to g out of the circle with them. Not knowing their custom, I supposed they designed to kill me, and refused to go. Then a grave Indian came and gave me a short pipe, and said in English, "Smoke it;" then he took me by the hand and led me out. My heart ached, thinking myself near my end. But he carried me to a French hut, about a mile from the Indian fort. The Frenchman was not at home, but his wife, who was a squaw, had some discourse with my Indian friend, which I did not understand. We tarried about two hours, then returned to the Indian village, where they gave me some victuals. Not long after this I saw one of my fellow-captives, who gave me a melancholy account of their sufferings after I left them.

After some weeks had passed, we left this village and went up St. John's river about ten miles, to a branch called *Medockscenecasis*, where there was one wigwam. At our arrival an old squaw saluted me with a yell, taking me by the hair and one hand, but

I was so rude as to break her hold and free myself. She gave me a filthy grin, and the Indians set up a laugh, and so it passed over.   Here we lived upon fish, wild grapes, roots, &c., which was hard living to me.

When the winter came on we went up the river till the ice came down, running thick in the river, when, according to the Indian custom, we laid up our canoes till spring.   Then we traveled sometimes on the ice, and sometimes on the land, till we came to a river that was open, but not fordable, where we made a raft and passed over, bag and baggage. I met with no abuse from them in this winter's hunting, though I was put to great hardships in carrying burdens and for want of food.   But they underwent the same difficulty, and would often encourage me, saying, in broken English, *" By and by great deal moose."*   Yet they could not answer any question I asked them.   And knowing little of their customs and way of life, I thought it tedious to be constantly moving from place to place, though it might be in some respects an advantage ; for it ran still in my mind that we were traveling to some settlement ; and when my burden was over-heavy, and the Indians left me behind, and the still evening coming on, I fancied I could see through the bushes and hear the people of some great town ; which hope, though some support to me in the day, yet I found not the town at night.

Thus we were hunting three hundred miles* from

---

* A pardonable error, perhaps, considering the author's ignorance of the geography of the country. He could hardly have got three hundred miles from the mouth of the Penobscot, in a northerly direction, without crossing the St. Lawrence.—S. G. Drake.

the sea, and knew no man within fifty or sixty miles
of us. We were eight or ten in number, and had but
two guns, on which we wholly depended for food. If
any disaster had happened, we must all have perished.
Sometimes we had no manner of sustenance for three
or four days; but God wonderfully provides for all
creatures. In one of these fasts, God's providence was
remarkable. Our two Indian men who had guns, in
hunting, started a moose, but there being a shallow
crusted snow on the ground, and the moose discovering
them, ran with great force into a swamp. The Indians
went round the swamp, and finding no track, returned
at night to the wigwam and told what had happened.
The next morning they followed him on the track and
soon found him lying on the snow. He had, in crossing the roots of a large tree that had been blown down,
broken through the ice made over the water in the
hole occasioned by the roots of the tree taking up the
ground, and hitched one of his hind legs among the
roots so fast that by striving to get it out, he pulled
his thigh-bone out of its socket at the hip, and thus
extraordinarily were we provided for in our great strait.
Sometimes they would take a bear, which go into dens
in the fall of the year without any sort of food, and lie
there four or five months without food, never going out
till spring, in which time they neither lose or gain in
flesh. If they went into their dens fat they came out
so, and if they went in lean they came out lean. I
have seen some which have come out with four whelps,
and both very fat, and then we feasted. An old squaw
and a captive, if any present, must stand without the

wigwam, shaking their hands and bodies, as in a dance, and singing, "WEGAGE OH NELO WOH," which in English is, "Fat is my eating." This is to signify their thankfulness in feasting times. When one supply was spent, we fasted till further success.

The way they preserve meat is by taking the flesh from the bones and drying it in smoke, by which it is kept sound months or years without salt. We moved still further up the country after moose when our store was out, so that by the spring we had got to the northward of the Lady mountains.* When the spring came and the rivers broke up, we moved back to the head of St. John's river, and there made canoes of moose hides, sewing three or four together and pitching the seams with balsam mixed with charcoal. Then we went down the river to a place called *Madawescook.†* There an old man lived and kept a sort of trading-house, where we tarried several days; then went further down the river till we came to the greatest falls in these parts, called Checanekepeag, where we carried a little way over the land, and putting off our canoes, we went down stream still. And as we passed down by the mouths of any large branches, we saw Indians; but when any dance was proposed, I was bought off. At length we arrived at the place where we left our birch canoes in the fall, and putting our baggage into them, went down to the fort.

---

* If these are the same the French called *Montz Notre Dame*, our captive was now on the borders of the St. Lawrence, to the north of the head of the bay of Chaleurs.— S. G. DRAKE.

† Probably the now well known Madawasca, of "disputed territory" memory.

There we planted corn, and after planting, went a fishing, and to look for and dig roots till the corn was fit to weed. After weeding, we took a second tour on the same errand, then returned to hill our corn. After hilling we went some distance from the fort and field, up the river, to take salmon and other fish, which we dried for food, where we continued till corn was filled with milk: some of it we dried then, the other as it ripened. To dry corn when in the milk, they gather it in large kettles and boil it on the ears, till it is pretty hard, then shell it from the cob with clam-shells, and dry it on bark in the sun. When it is thoroughly dry, a kernal is no bigger than a pea, and would keep years, and when it is boiled again it swells as large as when on the ear, and tastes incomparably sweeter than other corn. When we had gathered our corn and dried it in the way already described, we put some into Indian barns; that is, into holes in the ground, lined and covered with bark, and then with dirt. The rest we carried up the river upon our next winter's hunting.

Thus God wonderfully favored me, and carried me through the first year of my captivity.

CHAPTER II.

OF THE ABUSIVE AND BARBAROUS TREATMENT WHICH SEVERAL CAPTIVES MET WITH FROM THE INDIANS.

WHEN any great number of Indians met, or when any captives had been lately taken, or when any captives desert and are retaken, they have a dance, and torture the unhappy people who have fallen into their hands. My unfortunate brother, who was taken with me, after about three years' captivity, deserted with another Englishman, who had been taken from Casco Bay, and was retaken by the Indians at New Harbor, and carried back to Penobscot fort. Here they were both tortured at a stake by fire, for some time; then their noses and ears were cut off, and they made to eat them. After this they were burnt to death at the stake, the Indians at the same time declaring they would serve all deserters in the same manner. Thus they divert themselves in their dances.

On the second spring of my captivity, my Indian master and his squaw went to Canada, but sent me down the river with several Indians to the fort, to plant corn. The day before we came to the planting ground, we met two young Indian men who seemed to be in great haste. After they had passed us, I understood they were going with an express to Canada, and that there was an English vessel at the mouth of the river. I not being perfect in their language, nor knowing that English vessels traded with them in time of war, supposed a peace was concluded on, and that the captives would be released. I was so transported with this fancy, that I slept but little if any that night. Early the next morning we came to the village, where my ecstacy ended; for I had no sooner landed, but three or four Indians dragged me to the great wigwam, where they were yelling and dancing round James Alexander, a Jersey man, who was taken from Falmouth, in Casco Bay. This was occasioned by two families of Cape Sable Indians, who, having lost some friends by a number of English fishermen, came some hundreds of miles to revenge themselves on poor captives. They soon came to me and tossed me about till I was almost breathless, and then threw me into the ring to my fellow captive, and taking him out repeated their barbarities on him. Then I was hauled out again by three Indians, who seized me by the hair of the head, and bending me down by my hair, one beat me on the back and shoulders so long that my breath was almost beat out of my body. Then others put a *tomhake*[a] [tomahawk] into my hands, and ordered me to get up and sing and dance Indian, which I performed with the greatest reluctance, and while in the act, seemed determined to purchase my death by killing two or three of those monsters of cruelty, thinking it impossible to survive their bloody treatment; but it was impressed on my mind that it was not in their power to take away my life, so I desisted.

Then those Cape Sable Indians came to me again like bears bereaved of their whelps, saying, " Shall we who have lost relations by the English, suffer an English voice to be heard among us?" &c. Then they beat me again with the axe. Now I repented that I

[a] The *tomhake* is a warlike club, the shape of which may be seen in cuts of Etowonkoam, one of the four Indian chiefs, which cuts are common among us. [Mr. Gyles refers to the four Iroquois chiefs who visited England in the reign of Queen Anne. About those chiefs I have collected and published the particulars in the Book of the Indians. And I will here remark that the compilers of the ponderous Indian Biography and History, now in course of publication under the names of James Hall and T. L. McKenny, have *borrowed* my labors with no sparing hand—they have not even owned it, having no faith, probably, that by so doing they *might* pay half the debt. " He who steals my purse steals trash," but he who robs me of my labors * * —S. G. DRAKE.]

had not sent two or three of them out of the world before me, for I thought I had much rather die than suffer any longer. They left me the second time, and the other Indians put the tomhake into my hands again and compelled me to sing. Then I seemed more resolute than before to destroy some of them ; but a strange and strong impulse that I should return to my own place and people suppressed it as often as such a motion rose in my breast. Not one of them showed the least compassion, but I saw the tears run down plentifully on the cheeks of a Frenchman who sat behind, though it did not relieve the tortures that poor James and I were forced to endure for the most part of this tedious day, for they were continued till the evening, and were the most severe that ever I met with in the whole six years that I was a captive with the Indians.

After they had thus inhumanly abused us, two Indians took us up and threw us out of the wigwam, and we crawled away on our hands and feet, and were scarce able to walk for several days. Some time after they again concluded on a merry dance when I was at some distance from the wigwam dressing leather, and an Indian was so kind as to tell me that they had got James Alexander, and were in search for me. My Indian master and his squaw bid me run for my life into a swamp and hide, and not to discover myself unless they both came to me, for then I might be assured the dance was over. I was now master of their language, and a word or a wink was enough to excite me to take care of one. I ran to the swamp and hid in the thickest place I could find. I heard hallooing and whooping all around me; sometimes some passed very near me, and I could hear some threaten and others flatter me, but I was not disposed to dance. If they had come upon me, I had resolved to show them a pair of heels, and they must have had good luck to have catched me. I heard no more of them till about evening, for I think I slept, when they came again, calling, "Chon! Chon!" but John would not trust them. After they were gone, my master and his squaw came where they told me to hide, but could not find me; and when I heard them say, with some concern, they believed the other Indians had frightened me into the woods and that I was lost, I came out, and they seemed well pleased. They told me James had a bad day of it; that as soon as he was released he ran away into the woods, and they believed he was gone to the Mohawks. James soon returned and gave a melancholy account of his sufferings, and the Indians fright concerning the Mohawks. They often had terrible apprehensions of the incursions of those Indians. They are called also *Maquas*, a most ambitious, haughty, and blood-thirsty people, from whom the other Indians take their measures and manners, and their modes and changes of dress, &c. One very hot season, a great number gathered together at the village, and being a very droughty [thirsty] people, they kept James and myself night and day fetching water from a cold spring that ran out of a rocky hill about three-quarters of a mile from the fort. In going thither, we crossed a large interval cornfield, and then a descent to a lower interval before we ascended the hill to the spring. James being almost

4

dead, as well as I, with this continual fatigue, contrived to frighten the Indians. He told me of his plan, but conjured me to secrecy, yet said he knew I could keep counsel! The next dark night, James, going for water, set his kettle down on the descent to the lowest interval, and running back to the fort, puffing and blowing as though in the utmost surprise, told his master that he saw something near the spring that looked like Mohaws (which were only stumps). His master, being a most courageous warrior, went with him to make discovery. When they came to the brow of the hill, James pointed to the stumps, and withal touching his kettle with his toe, gave it motion down the hill; at every turn its bail clattered, which caused James and his master to see a Mohawk in every stump, and they lost no time in "turning tail to," and he was the best fellow who could run the fastest. This alarmed all the Indians in the village. They were about thirty or forty in number, and they packed off, bag and baggage, some up the river and others down, and did not return under fifteen days; and then the heat of the weather being finally over, our hard service was abated for this season. I never heard that the Indians understood the occasion of their fright: but James and I had many a private laugh about it.

But my most intimate and dear companion was one John Evans, a young man taken from Quochecho. We, as often as we could, met together and made known our grievances to each other, which seemed to ease our minds; but as soon as it was known to the Indians, we were strictly examined apart, and falsely accused of contriving to desert. We were too far from the sea to have any thought of that, and finding our stories agreed, did not punish us. An English captive girl about this time, who was taken by Medocawando, would often falsely accuse us of plotting to desert, but we made the truth so plainly appear, that she was checked and we were released. But the third winter of my captivity, John Evans went into the country, and the Indians imposed a heavy burden on him while he was extremely weak from long fasting; and as he was going off the upland over a place of ice, which was very hollow, he broke through, fell down, and cut his knee very much. Notwithstanding, he traveled for some time, but the wind and cold were so forcible that they soon overcame him, and he sat or fell down, and all the Indians passed by him. Some of them went back the next day, after him or his pack, and found him, with a dog in his arms, both frozen to death. Thus all of my fellow-captives were dispersed and dead, but through infinite and unmerited goodness I was supported under and carried through all difficulties.

CHAPTER III.

OF FURTHER DIFFICULTIES AND DELIVERANCES.

ONE winter, as we were moving from place to place, our hunters killed some moose. One lying some miles from our wigwams, a young Indian and myself were ordered to fetch part of it. We set out in the morning, when the weather was promising, but it proved a very cold, cloudy day. It was late in the evening before we arrived at the place where the moose lay, so that we had no time to provide materials for fire or shelter. At the same time came on a storm of snow, very thick, which continued until the next morning. We made a small fire with what little rubbish we could find around us. The fire, with the warmth of our bodies, melted the snow upon us as fast as it fell, and so our clothes were filled with water. However, early in the morning we took our loads of moose flesh, and set out on our return to our wigwams. We had not gone far before my moose-skin coat (which was the only garment I had on my back, and the hair chiefly worn off), was frozen stiff round my knees like a hoop, as were my snow-shoes and snow-clouts to my feet. Thus I marched the whole day without fire or food. At first I was in great pain, then my flesh became numb, and at times I felt extremely sick, and thought I could not travel one foot further, but I wonderfully revived again.

After long traveling I felt very drowsy, and had thoughts of sitting down, which had I done, without doubt I had fallen on my last sleep, as my dear companion, Evans, had done before. My Indian companion, being better clothed, had left me long before. Again my spirits revived as much as if I had received the richest cordial. Some hours after sunset I reached the wigwam, and crawling in with my snow-shoes on, the Indians cried out, " The captive is frozen to death." They took off my pack, and the place where they lay against my back was the only one that was not frozen. They cut off my snow shoes and stripped off the clouts

from my feet, which were as void of feeling as any
frozen flesh could be. I had not sat long by the fire
before the blood began to circulate, and my feet to my
ankles turned black, and swelled with bloody blisters,
and were inexpressibly painful. The Indians said one
to another, " His feet will rot and he will die.' Yet
I slept well at night. Soon after, the skin came off my
feet from my ankles, whole, like a shoe, leaving my toes
naked without a nail, and the ends of my great toe
bones bare, which, in a little time turned black, so that
I was obliged to cut the first joint off with my knife.
The Indians gave me rags to bind up my feet, and
advised me to apply fir balsam, but withal added that
they believed it was not worth while to use means, for
I should certainly die. But, by the use of my elbows
and a stick in each hand, I shoved myself along as I
sat upon the ground over the snow from one tree to
another, till I got some balsam. This I burned in a
clam-shell till it was of a consistence like salve, which
I applied to my feet and ankles, and, by the divine
blessing, within a week I could go about upon my heels
with my staff. And, through God's goodness, we had
provisions enough, so that we did not remove under
ten or fifteen days. Then the Indians made two little
hoops, something in the form of a snow-shoe, and sewing them to my feet, I was able to follow them in their
tracks, on my heels, from place to place, though sometimes half leg deep in snow and water, which gave me
the most acute pain imaginable; but I must walk or
die. Yet within a year my feet were entirely well;
and the nails came on my great toes, so that a very

critical eye could scarcely perceive any part missing, or that they had been frozen at all.

In a time of great scarcity of provisions, the Indians chased a large moose into the river, and killed him. They brought the flesh to the village and raised it on a scaffold, in a large wigwam, in order to make a feast. I was very officious in supplying them with wood and water, which pleased them so well that they now and then gave me a piece of flesh half boiled or roasted, which I ate with eagerness, and I doubt not without due thankfulness to the divine Being who so extraordinarily fed me. At length the scaffold bearing the moose meat broke, and I being under it, a large piece fell and knocked me on the head.[*] The Indians said I lay stunned a considerable time. The first I was sensible of, was a murmuring noise in my ears, then my sight gradually returned, with an extreme pain in my hand, which was very much bruised; and it was long before I recovered, the weather being very hot.

I was once fishing with an Indian for sturgeon, and the Indian darting one, his feet slipped, and he turned the canoe bottom upward with me under it. I held fast to the cross-bar, as I could not swim, with my face to the bottom of the canoe, but turning myself, I brought my breast to bear on the cross-bar, expecting every minute the Indian to tow me to the bank. But " he had other fish to fry." Thus I continued a quarter of an hour; [though] without want of breath, till

---

[*] Whether he were struck by a timber of the scaffold, or a quantity of the meat on it, we are left to conjecture, and it is not very material:—S. G. DRAKE.

the current drove me on a rocky point where I could reach bottom. There I stopped and turned up my canoe. On looking about for the Indian, I saw him half a mile off up the river. On going to him, I asked him why he had not towed me to the bank, seeing he knew I could not swim. He said he knew I was under the canoe, for there were no bubbles any where to be seen, and that I should drive on the point. So while he was taking care of his fine sturgeon, which was eight or ten feet in length, I was left to sink or swim.

Once, as we were fishing for salmon at a fall of about fifteen feet of water, I came near being drownded in a deep hole at the foot of the fall. The Indians went into the water to wash themselves, and asked me to go with them. I told them I could not swim, but they insisted, and so I went in. They ordered me to dive across the deepest place, and if I fell short of the other side they said they would help me. But, instead of diving across the narrowest part, I was crawling on the bottom into the deepest place. They not seeing me rise, and knowing whereabouts I was by the bubbling of the water, a young girl dived down and brought me up by the hair, otherwise I had perished in the water. Though the Indians, both male and female, go into the water together, they have each of them such covering on that not the least indecency can be observed, and neither chastity nor modesty is violated.

While at the Indian village, I had been cutting wood and binding it up with an Indian rope, in order to carry it to the wigwam, a stout, ill-natured young fellow, about twenty years of age, threw me backward, sat on my breast, pulled out his knife, and said he would kill me, for he had never yet killed one of the English. I told him he might go to war, and that would be more manly than to kill a poor captive who was doing their drudgery for them. Notwithstanding all I could say, he began to cut and stab me on my breast. I seized him by the hair, and tumbling him off of me, followed him with my fists and knee with such application that he soon cried "enough." But when I saw the blood run from my bosom, and felt the smart of the wounds he had given me, I at him again, and bid him get up and not lie there like a dog: told him of his former abuses offered to me and other poor captives, and that if ever he offered the like to me again, I would pay him double. I sent him before me, and taking up my burden of wood, came to the Indians and told them the whole truth, and they commended me. And I do not remember that ever he offered me the least abuse afterwards, though he was big enough to have despatched two of me.

CHAPTER IV.

OF REMARKABLE EVENTS OF PROVIDENCE IN THE DEATHS OF SEVERAL BARBAROUS INDIANS.

THE priest of this river was of the order of Saint Francis, a gentleman of a humane and generous disposition. In his sermons he most severely reprehended the Indians for their barbarities to captives. He would often tell them that, excepting their errors in religion, the English were a better people than themselves, and that God would remarkably punish such cruel wretches, and had begun to execute his vengeance upon such already! He gave an account of the retaliations of Providence upon those murderous Cape Sable Indians above mentioned, one of whom got a splinter into his foot, which festered and rotted his flesh till it killed him. Another run a fish-bone into her hand or arm, and she rotted to death, notwithstanding all means that were used to prevent it. In some such manner they all died, so that not one of those two families lived to return home.[*] Were it not for these remarks of the priest, I had not, perhaps, have noticed these providences.

There was an old squaw who ever endeavored to outdo all others in cruelty to captives. Wherever she came into a wigwam, where any poor, naked, starved captives were sitting near the fire, if they were grown persons, she would stealthily take up a shovel of hot coals and throw them into their bosoms. If they were young persons, she would seize them by the hand or leg, drag them through the fire, &c. The Indians with whom she lived, according to their custom, left their village in the fall of the year, and dispersed themselves for hunting. After the first or second removal, they all strangely forgot that old squaw and her grandson, about twelve years of age. They were found dead in the place where they were left, some months afterwards,

---

[*] Reference is probably had to those Indians of whom the author has before spoken as having come to the fort of those with whom he was among, to be revenged on any whites for the loss of some of their friends who had been killed by white fishermen. —S. G. DRAKE.

and no further notice was taken of them by their friends. Of this the priest made special remark, forasmuch as it is a thing very uncommon for them to neglect either their old or young people.

In the latter part of summer or beginning of autumn, the Indians were frequently frightened by the appearance of strange Indians passing up and down this river in canoes, and about that time the next year died more than one hundred persons, old and young, all, or most of those who saw those strange Indians! The priest said it was a sort of plague. A person seeming in perfect health would bleed at the mouth and nose, turn blue in spots, and die in two or three hours.* It was very tedious to me to remove from place to place this cold season. The Indians applied red ochre to my sores [which had been occasioned by the affray before mentioned], which by God's blessing cured me. This sickness being at the worst as winter came on, the Indians all scattered, and the blow was so great to them, that they did not settle or plant at their village while I was on the river [St. Johns], and I know not whether they have to this day. Before they thus deserted the village, when they came in from hunting, they would be drunk and fight for several days and nights together, till they had spent most of their skins in wine and brandy, which was brought to the village by a Frenchman called Monsieur *Sigenioncour.*

---

* Calamitous mortalities are often mentioned as happening among the Indians, but that the appearance of strange Indians had anything to do with it, will only excite admiration to the enlightened of this age. It was by a mortality something similar that the country about the coast of Massachusetts was nearly depopulated two or three years before the settlement of Plymouth.—S. G. DRAKE.

CHAPTER V.

OF THEIR FAMILIARITY WITH, AND FRIGHTS FROM, THE DEVIL, ETC.

THE Indians are very often surprised with the appearance of ghosts and demons. Sometimes they are encouraged by the devil, for they go to him for success in hunting. &c. I was once hunting with Indians who were not brought over to the Romish faith, and after several days they proposed to inquire, according to their custom, what success they should have. They accordingly prepared many hot stones, and laying them in a heap, made a small hut covered with skins and mats; then, in a dark night two of the powwows went into this hot house with a large vessel of water, which at times they poured on those hot rocks, which raised a thick steam, so that a third Indian was obliged to stand without, and lift up a mat to give it vent when they were almost suffocated. There was an old squaw who was kind to captives, and never joined with them in their powwowing, to whom I manifested an earnest desire to see their management. She told me that if they knew of my being there they would kill me, and that when she was a girl she had known young persons to be taken away by a hairy man, and therefore she would not advise me to go, lest the hairy man should carry me away. I told her I was not afraid of the hairy man, nor could he hurt me if she would not

discover me to the powwows. At length she promised
me she would not, but charged me to be careful of
myself. I went within three or four feet of the hot
house, for it was very dark, and heard strange noises
and yellings, such as I never heard before. At times
the Indian who tended without would lift up the mat,
and a steam would issue which looked like fire. I lay
there two or three hours, but saw none of their hairy
men or demons. And when I found they had finished
their ceremony, I went to the wigwam and told the
squaw what had passed. She was glad I had escaped
without hurt, and never discovered what I had done.
After some time inquiry was made of the powwows
what success we were likely to have in our hunting.
They said they had very likely signs of success, but no
real ones as at other times. A few days after, we
moved up the river and had pretty good luck.

One afternoon as I was in a canoe with one of the
powwows, the dog barked, and presently a moose
passed by within a few rods of us, so that the waves
he made by wading rolled our canoe. The Indian
shot at him, but the moose took very little notice of it,
and went into the woods to the southward. The fellow said, "I will try if I can't fetch you back for all
your haste." The evening following we built our two
wigwams on a sandy point on the upper end of an
island in the river, northwest of the place where the
moose went into the woods, and here the Indian pow-
wowed the greatest part of the night following. In
the morning we had a fair track of a moose round our
wigwams, though we did not see or taste of it. I am

of opinion that the devil was permitted to humor those
unhappy wretches sometimes, in some things.*

That it may appear how much they were deluded,
or under the influence of satan, read the two stories
which were related and believed by the Indians. The
first, of a boy who was carried away by a large bird
called a *Gulloua*, who buildeth his nest on a high rock
or mountain. A boy was hunting with his bow and
arrow at the foot of a rocky mountain, when the gulloua came diving through the air, grasped the boy in
her talons, and although he was eight or ten years of
age, she soared aloft and laid him in her nest, food for
her young. The boy lay still on his face, but observed
two of the young birds in the nest with him having
much fish and flesh to feed upon. The old bird seeing
they would not eat the boy, took him up in her claws
and returned him to the place from whence she took
him. I have passed near the mountain in a canoe,
and the Indians have said, "There is the nest of the
great bird that carried away the boy." Indeed, there
seemed to be a great number of sticks put together like
a nest, on the top of the mountain. At another time
they said, "There is the bird, but he is now as a boy
to a giant to what he was in former days." The bird
which we saw was a large and speckled one, like an
eagle, though somewhat larger.†

* Whatever the Indians might have believed about the devil, one thing is pretty
clear, that our captive had great faith in his abilities. Quite as easy a way to have
accounted for moose tracks about their wigwam, would have been to suppose that that
animal might have been attracted by the uncouth noise of the powwow to approach
them for the object of discovery. It is very common for wild animals to do so.—S. G.
DRAKE.

† Not exactly a *fish story*, but it is certainly a *bird story*, and although Mr. Gyles has

When from the mountain tops, with hideous cry
And clattering wings, the hungry harpies fly,
They snatched   *   *   *   *
*   *   And whether gods or birds obscene they were,
Our vows for pardon and for peace prefer.

DRYDEN'S VIRGIL.

The other notion is, that a young Indian in his hunting, was belated, and losing his way, was on a sudden introduced to a large wigwam full of dried eels, which proved to be a beaver's house, in which he lived till the spring of the year, when he was turned out of the house, and being set upon a beaver's dam, went home and related the affair to his friends at large.

CHAPTER VI.

A DESCRIPTION OF SEVERAL CREATURES COMMONLY TAKEN BY THE INDIANS ON ST. JOHN'S RIVER.

I. *Of the Beaver.*—The beaver has a very thick, strong neck; his fore teeth, which are two in the upper and two in the under jaw, are concave and sharp like a carpenter's gouge. Their side teeth are like a sheep's, for they chew the cud. Their legs are short, the claws something longer than in other creatures. The nails on the toes of their hind feet are flat like an ape's, but joined together by a membrane, as those of the water-fowl, their tails broad and flat like the broad end of a paddle. Near their tails they have four bottles, two

---

fortified himself behind " believed by the Indians," yet I fear his reputation for credulity will be somewhat enhanced in the mind of the reader. I think, however, it should not derogate from his character for veracity.—S. G. DRAKE.

of which contain oil, the others gum; the necks of these meet in one common orifice. The latter of these bottles contain the proper castorum, and not the testicles, as some have fancied, for they are distinct and separate from them, in the males only; whereas the castorum and oil bottles are common to male and female. With this oil and gum they preen themselves, so that when they come out of the water it runs off of them as it does from a fowl. They have four teats, which are on their breasts, so that they hug up their young and suckle them as women do their infants. They have generally two, and sometimes four in a litter. I have seen seven or five in the matrix, but the Indians think it a strange thing to find so many in a litter; and they assert that when it so happens, the dam kills all but four. They are the most laborious creatures that I have met with. I have known them to build dams across a river thirty or forty perches wide, with wood and mud, so as to flow many acres of land. In the deepest part of a pond so raised, they build their houses, round, in the figure of an Indian wigwam, eight or ten feet high, and six or eight in diameter on the floor, which is made descending to the water, the parts near the centre about four, and near the circumference, between ten and twenty inches above the water. These floors are covered with strippings of wood, like shavings. On these they sleep with their tails in the water;[*] and if the freshets rise, they have

---

[*] I recollect to have seen a similar statement by that singular genius, Thomas Morton, of Mare Mount, in his more singular book, New English Canaan, about beavers keeping their tails in the water. Morton, however, tells us the reason they do so, viz: "which else would overheat and rot off."—S. G. DRAKE.

the advantage of rising on their floor to the highest part. They feed on the leaves and bark of trees, and pond-lily roots. In the fall of the year they lay in their provision for the approaching winter, cutting down trees great and small. With one end in their mouths they drag their branches near to their house, and sink many cords of it. (They will cut [gnaw] down trees of a fathom in circumference.) They have doors to go down to the wood under the ice. And in case the freshets rise, break down and carry off their store of wood, they often starve. They have a note for conversing, calling, and warning each other when at work or feeding; and while they are at labor they keep out a guard, who, upon the first approach of an enemy, so strikes the water with his tail that he may be heard half a mile. This so alarms the rest that they are all silent, quit their labor, and are to be seen no more for that time. If the male or female die, the survivor seeks a mate and conducts him or her to their house, and carry on affairs as above.

II. *Of the Wolverene.* [*Gulo Luscus* of L.] The wolverene is a very fierce and mischievous creature, about the bigness of a middling dog, having short legs, broad feet, and very sharp claws, and in my opinion may be reckoned a species of cat. They will climb trees and wait for moose and other animals which feed below, and when opportunity presents, jump upon and strike their claws in them so fast that they will hang on them till they have gnawed the main nerve in their neck asunder, which causes their death. I have known many moose killed thus. I was once traveling a little way behind several Indians, and hearing them laugh merrily, when I came up I asked them the cause of their laughter. They showed me the track of a moose, and how a wolverene had climbed a tree, and where he had jumped off upon a moose. It so happened, that after the moose had taken several large leaps, it came under the branch of a tree, which striking the wolverene, broke his hold and tore him off; and by his tracks in the snow it appeared he went off another way, with short steps, as if he had been stunned by the blow that had broken his hold. The Indians imputed the accident to the cunning of the moose, and were wonderfully pleased that it had thus outwitted the mischievous wolverene.

These wolverenes go into wigwams which have been left for a time, scatter the things abroad, and most filthily pollute them with ordure. I have heard the Indians say that this animal has sometimes pulled their guns from under their heads while they were asleep, and left them so defiled. An Indian told me that having left his wigwam, with sundry things on the scaffold, among which was a birchen flask containing several pounds of powder, he found at his return, much to his surprise and grief, that a wolverene had visited it, mounted the scaffold, hove down bag and baggage. The powder flask happening to fall into the fire, exploded, blowing up the wolverene, and scattering the wigwam in all directions. At length he found the creature, blind from the blast, wandering backward and forward, and he had the satisfaction of kicking and beating him about. This, in a great measure, made

6

up their loss, and then they could contentedly pick up
their utensils and rig out their wigwam.

III. *Of the Hedgehog* [*Histrix Dorsata*], *or Urchin*
[*Urson?*] Our hedgehog, or urchin, is about the bigness of a hog six months old. His back, sides, and
tail are full of sharp quills, so that if any creature approach him, he will contract himself into a globular
form, and when touched by his enemy, his quills are
so sharp and loose in the skin they fix in the mouth of
the adversary. They will strike with great force with
their tails, so that whatever falls under the lash of them
are certainly filled with their prickles ; but that they
shoot their quills, as some assert they do, is a great
mistake, as respects the American hedgehog, and I
believe as to the African hedgehog or porcupine, also.
As to the former, I have taken them at all seasons of
the year.

IV. *Of the Tortoise.* It is needless to describe the
fresh-water tortoise, whose form is so well known in all
parts ; but their manner of propagating their species is
not so universally known. I have observed that sort
of tortoise whose shell is about fourteen or sixteen
inches wide. In their coition they may be heard half
a mile, making a noise like a woman washing her linen
with a batting staff. They lay their eggs in the sand,
near some deep, still water, about a foot beneath the
surface of the sand, with which they are very curious in
covering them ; so that there is not the least mixture of
it amongst them, nor the least rising of sand on the
beach where they are deposited. I have often searched
for them with the Indians, by thrusting a stick into the

sand at random, and brought up some part of an egg clinging to it: when uncovering the place, we have found near one hundred and fifty in one nest. Both their eggs and flesh are good eating when boiled. I have observed a difference as to the length of time in which they are hatching, which is between twenty and thirty days, some sooner than others. Whether this difference ought to be imputed to the various quality or site of the sand in which they are laid (as to the degree of cold or heat), I leave to the conjecture of the virtuosi. As soon as they are hatched, the young tortoise breaks through the sand and betake themselves to the water, and, as far as I could discover, without any further care or help of the old ones.

CHAPTER VII.

OF THEIR FEASTING.

1. *Before they go to war.* When the Indians determine on war, or are entering on a particular expedition, they kill a number of their dogs, burn off the hair, and cut them to pieces, leaving only one dog's head whole. The rest of the flesh they boil, and make a fine feast of it. Then the dog's head that was left whole is scorched till the nose and lips have shrunk from the teeth, leaving them bare and grinning. This done, they fasten it on a stick, and the Indian who is proposed to be chief in the expedition, takes the head into his hand and sings a warlike song, in which he mentions the town they design to attack, and the prin-

cipal man in it, threatening that in a few days he will carry that man's head and scalp in his hand in the same manner. When the chief has finished singing, he so places the dog's head as to grin at him who he supposes will go his second, who, if he accepts, takes the head in his hand and sings; but if he refuses to go he turns the teeth to another; and thus from one to another till they have enlisted their company.

The Indians imagine that dog's flesh makes them bold and courageous. I have seen an Indian split a dog's head with a hatchet, take out the brains hot, and eat them raw with the blood running down his jaws !

2. *When a relation dies.* In a still evening, a squaw will walk on the highest land near her abode, and with a loud and mournful voice will exclaim, " *Oh! hawe, hawe, hawe,*" with a long mournful tone to each *hawe,* for a long time together. After the mourning season is over, the relations of the deceased make a feast to wipe off tears, and the bereaved may marry freely. If the deceased was a squaw, the relations consult together and choose a squaw (doubtless a widow), and send her to the widower, and if he likes her he takes her to be his wife, if not, he sends her back, and the relations choose and send till they find one that he approves of.

If a young fellow determines to marry, his relations and a Jesuit advise him to a girl. He goes into the wigwam where she is, and looks on her. If he likes her appearance, he tosses a stick or chip into her lap, which she takes, and with a reserved, side look, views the person who sent it, yet handles the chip with admiration, as though she wondered from whence it came.

If she likes him she throws the chip to him with a modest smile, and then nothing is wanting but a ceremony with the Jesuit to consummate the marriage. But if she dislikes her suitor, she, with a surly countenance, throws the chip aside, and he comes no more there.

If parents have a daughter marriageable, they seek a husband for her who is a good hunter. If she has been educated to make *monoodah* (Indian bags), birch dishes, to lace snow shoes, make Indian shoes, string wampum belts, sew birch canoes, and boil the kettle, she is esteemed a lady of fine accomplishments. If the man sought out for her husband have a gun and ammunition, a canoe, a spear, a hatchet, a monoodah, a crooked knife, looking-glass and paint, a pipe, tobacco, and knot-bowl to toss a kind of dice in, he is accounted a gentleman of a plentiful fortune. Whatever the new married man procures the first year belongs to his wife's parents. If the young pair have a child within a year and nine months, they are thought to be very forward and libidinous persons.

By their play with dice they lose much time, playing whole days and nights together, sometimes staking their whole effects, though this is accounted a great vice by the old men.

A digression.—There is an old story told among the Indians of a family who had a daughter that was accounted a finished beauty, having been adorned with the precious jewel, an Indian education! She was so formed by nature and polished by art, that they could not find for her a suitable consort. At length, while

this family were once residing upon the head of Penobscot river, under the White Hills, called *Teddon*, this
fine creature was missing, and her parents could learn
no tidings of her.   After much time and pains spent,
and tears showered in quest of her, they saw her divert-
ing herself with a beautiful youth, whose hair, like her
own, flowed down below his waist, swimming, washing,
&c., in the water ; but they vanished on their approach.
This beautiful person, whom they imagined to be one
of those kind spirits who inhabit the Teddon, they
looked upon as their son-in-law ; and, according to
their custom, they called upon him for moose, bear, or
whatever creature they desired, and if they did but go
to the water-side and signify their desire, the animal
would come swimming to them !   I have heard an
Indian say that he lived by the river, at the foot of
the Teddon, the top of which he could see through the
hole of his wigwam left for the smoke to pass out.   He
was tempted to travel to it, and accordingly set out on
a summer morning, and labored hard in ascending the
hill, all day, and the top seemed as distant from the
place where he lodged at night as from his wigwam,
where he began his journey.   He now concluded the
spirits were there, and never dared to make a second
attempt.

   I have been credibly informed that several others
have failed in like attempts.   Once three young men
climbed towards its summit three days and a half, at
the end of which time they became strangely disor-
dered with delirium, &c., and when their imagination
was clear, and they could recollect where they were,

they found themselves returned one day's journey. How they came to be thus transported they could not conjecture, unless the genii of the place had conveyed them. These White Hills, at the head of Penobscot river, are, by the Indians, said to be much higher than those called Agiockochhook, above Saco.*

But to return to an Indian feast, of which you may request a bill of fare before you go. If you dislike it, stay at home. The ingredients are fish, flesh, or Indian corn and beans boiled together; sometimes hasty pudding made of pounded corn, whenever and as often as these are plenty. An Indian boils four or five large kettles full, and sends a messenger to each wigwam door, who exclaims, "*Kuh menscoorebah!*" that is, "I come to conduct you to a feast." The man within demands whether he must take a spoon or a knife in his dish, which he always carries with him. They appoint two or three young men to mess it out, to each man his portion, according to the number of his family at home. This is done with the utmost exactness. When they have done eating, a young fellow stands without the door and cries aloud, "*Mensecommook!*" "come and fetch!" Immediately each squaw goes to her husband and takes what he has left, which she carries home and eats with her children. For neither married women, nor any youth under twenty, are allowed to be present: but old widow squaws and captive men may sit by the door. The Indian men continue in the wigwam, some relating their warlike exploits, others something comical, others narrating their hunting exploits. The seniors gave maxims of prudence and grave counsel to the young men; and though every one's speech be agreeable to the run of his own fancy, yet they confine themselves to rule, and but one speaks at a time. After every man has told his story, one rises up, sings a feast song, and others succeed alternately as the company sees fit.

Necessity is the mother of invention. If an Indian loses his fire, he can presently take two sticks, one harder than the other (the drier the better), and in the softest one make a hollow or socket, in which one end of the hardest stick being inserted, then holding the softest piece firm between his knees, whirls it round like a drill, and fire will kindle in a few minutes.

If they have lost or left their kettle, it is but putting their victuals into a birch dish, leaving a vacancy in the middle, filling it with water, and putting in hot stones alternately; they will thus thoroughly boil the toughest neck of beef.

CHAPTER VIII.

OF MY THREE YEARS CAPTIVITY WITH THE FRENCH.

WHEN about six years of my doleful captivity had passed, my second Indian master died, whose squaw and my first Indian master disputed whose slave I should be. Some malicious persons advised them to end the quarrel by putting a period to my life; but honest father Simon, the priest of the river, told them

that it would be a heinous crime, and advised them to
sell me to the French. There came annually one or
two men of war to supply the fort, which was on the
river about thirty-four leagues from the sea. The Indians having advice of the arrival of a man of war at
the mouth of the river, they, about thirty or forty in
number, went on board ; for the gentlemen from France
made a present to them every year, and set forth the
riches and victories of their monarch, &c. At this
time they presented the Indians with a bag or two of
flour with some prunes, as ingredients for a feast. I,
who was dressed up in an old greasy blanket, without
cap, hat, or shirt (for I had had no shirt for the six
years except the one I had on at the time I was made
prisoner), was invited into the great cabin, where
many well-rigged gentlemen were sitting, who would
fain have had a full view of me. I endeavored to
hide myself behind the hangings, for I was much
ashamed, thinking how I had once worn clothes, and
of my living with people who could rig as well as the
best of them. My master asked me whether I chose
to be sold to the people of the man of war, or to the
inhabitants of the country. I replied, with tears, that
I should be glad if he would sell me to the English
from whom I was taken ; but that if I must be sold to
the French, I wished to be sold to the lowest inhabitants on the river, or those nearest to the sea, who were
about twenty-five leagues from the mouth of the river :
for I thought if I were sold to the gentlemen in the
ship, I should never return to the English.

This was the first time I had seen the sea during my

7

captivity, and the first time that I had tasted salt or bread.

My master presently went on shore, and a few days after, all the Indians went up the river. When we came to a house which I had spoken to my master about, he went on shore with me and tarried all night. The master of the house spoke kindly to me in Indian, for I could not then speak one word of French. Madam also looked pleasant on me, and gave me some bread. The next day I was sent six leagues further up the river to another French house. My master and the friar tarried with Monsieur Dechouffour, the gentleman who had entertained us the night before. Not long after, father Simon came and said, " Now you are one of us, for you are sold to that gentleman by whom you were entertained the other night." I replied, " Sold ! to a Frenchman !" I could say no more, went into the woods alone, and wept till I could scarce see or stand ! The word *sold*, and that to a people of that persuasion which my dear mother so much detested, and in her last words manifested so great fears of my falling into ! These thoughts almost broke my heart.

When I had thus given vent to my grief I wiped my eyes, endeavoring to conceal its effects, but father Simon, perceiving my eyes were swollen, called me aside, and bidding me not to grieve, for the gentleman, he said, to whom I was sold was of a good humor ; that he had formerly bought two captives, both of whom had been sent to Boston. This, in some measure, revived me ; but, he added, he did not suppose I would ever wish to go to the English, for the French religion was so much better. He said, also, he should pass that way in about ten days, and if I did not like to live with the French better than with the Indians, he would buy me again. On the day following, father Simon and my Indian master went up the river six and thirty leagues, to their chief village, and I went down the river six leagues with two Frenchmen to my new master. He kindly received me, and in a few days madam made me an osnaburg shirt and French cap, and a coat out of one of my master's old coats. Then I threw away my greasy blanket and Indian flap, and looked as smart as ———. And I never more saw the old friar, the Indian village, or my Indian master, till about fourteen years after, when I saw my old Indian master at Port Royal, whither I had been sent by the government with a flag of truce for the exchange of prisoners; and again, about twenty-four years since, he came to St. Johns, to fort George, to see me, where I made him very welcome.

My French master held a great trade with the Indians, which suited me very well, I being thorough in the languages of the tribes at Cape Sable and St. Johns.

I had not lived long with this gentleman before he committed to me the keys of his store, &c., and my whole employment was trading and hunting, in which I acted faithfully for my master, and never, knowingly, wronged him to the value of one farthing.

They spoke to me so much in Indian that it was some time before I was perfect in the French tongue. Monsieur generally had his goods from the men of war which came there annually from France.

In the year 1696, two men of war came to the mouth of the river. In their way they had captured the Newport, Captain Payson, and brought him with them. They made the Indians some presents, and invited them to join in an expedition to Pemmaquid. They accepted it, and soon after arrived there. Captain Chubb, who commanded that post, delivered it up without much dispute, to Monsieur D'Iberville, as I heard the gentleman say, with whom I lived, who was there present.*

Early in the spring I was sent with three Frenchmen to the mouth of the river, for provision, which came from Port Royal. We carried over land from the river to a large bay, where we were driven on an island by a northeast storm, where we were kept seven days, without any sustenance, for we expected a quick passage, and carried nothing with us. The wind continuing boisterous, we could not return back, and the ice prevented our going forward. After seven days the ice broke up and we went forward, though we were so weak that we could scarce hear each other speak. The people at the mouth of the river were

---

* The Reverend Dr. Mather says wittily, as he says everything, "This Chubb found opportunity, in a pretty Chubbish manner, to kill the famous Edgeremet and Abenquid, a couple of principal Indians, on a Lord's day, the 16th of February, 1695. If there is any unfair dealing in this action of Chubb, there will be another February, not far off, wherein the avenger of blood will take satisfaction."—Hist. N. E. [Magnalia] B. vii. 79.

Mr. Mather adds, "On the 4th or 5th of August, Chubb, with an uncommon baseness, did surrender the brave fort of Pemmaquid into their hands." [For an account of the wretched fate of Chubb as well as that of the whole transaction, see Book of the Indians, B. iii. 121, 122.]

Unthinking men no sort of scruples make,
And some are bad only for mischief's sake,
But ev'n the best are guilty by mistake.

surprised to see us alive, and advised us to be cautious and abstemious in eating. By this time I knew as much of fasting as they, and dieted on broth, and recovered very well, as did one of the others, but the other two would not be advised, and I never saw any persons in greater distress, till at length they had action of the bowels, when they recovered.

A friar, who lived in the family, invited me, to confession, but I excused myself as well as I could at that time. One evening he took me into his apartment in the dark and advised me to confess to him what sins I had committed. I told him I could not remember a thousandth part of them, they were so numerous. Then he bid me remember and relate as many as I could, and he would pardon them, signifying he had a bag to put them in. I told him I did not believe it was in the power of any but God to pardon sin. He asked me whether I had read the Bible. I told him I had when I was a little boy, but it was so long ago I had forgotten most of it. Then he told me he did not pardon my sins, but when he knew them he prayed to God to pardon them: when, perhaps, I was at my sports and plays. He wished me well, and hoped I should be better advised, and said he should call for me in a little time. Thus he dismissed me, nor did he ever call me to confession afterwards.

The gentleman with whom I lived had a fine field of wheat, in which great numbers of blackbirds continually collected and made great havoc in it. The French said a Jesuit would come and banish them. He did at length come, and having all things prepared, he took a basin of holy water, a staff with a little brush, and having on his white robe, went into the field of wheat. I asked several prisoners who had lately been taken by privateers, and brought in there, viz: Mr. Woodbury, Cocks [Cox?] and Morgan, whether they would go and see the ceremony. Mr. Woodbury asked me whether I designed to go, and I told him yes. He then said I was as bad as a papist, and a d—d fool. I told him I believed as little of it as he did, but I was inclined to see the ceremony, that I might tell it to my friends.

With about thirty following in procession, the Jesuit marched through the field of wheat, a young lad going before him bearing the holy water. Then the Jesuit, dipping his brush into the holy water, sprinkled the field on each side of him, a little bell jingling at the same time, and all singing the words, *Ora pro nobis.* At the end of the field they wheeled to the left about, and returned. Thus they passed and repassed the field of wheat, the blackbirds all the while rising before them only to light behind. At their return I told a French lad that the friar had done no service, and recommended them to shoot the birds. The lad left me, as I thought, to see what the Jesuit would say to my observation, which turned out to be the case, for he told the lad that the sins of the people were so great he could not prevail against those birds. The same friar as vainly attempted to banish the musketoes from Signecto, but the sins of the people there were also too great for him to prevail, but, on the other hand, it seemed that more came, which caused the people to suspect that some had come for the sins of the Jesuit also.

Some time after, Colonel Hawthorne attempted the taking of the French fort up this river. We heard of him some time before he came up. by the guard which Governor Villebon had stationed at the river's mouth. Monsieur, my master, had gone to France, and madam, his wife. advised with me. She desired me to nail a paper on the door of her house. which paper read as follows :

" I entreat the general of the English not to burn my house, or barn. nor destroy my cattle. I don't suppose that such an army comes here to destroy a few inhabitants. but to take the fort above us. I have shown kindness to the English captives, as we were capacitated. and have bought two. of the Indians, and sent them to Boston. We have one now with us, and he shall go also when a convenient opportunity presents. and he desires it."

When I had done this, madam said to me. " Little English." [which was the familiar name she used to call me by], " we have shown you kindness, and now it lies in your power to serve or disserve us, as you know where our goods are hid in the woods, and that monsieur is not at home. I could have sent you to the fort and put you under confinement, but my respect to you and your assurance of love to us have disposed me to confide in you, persuaded you will not hurt us or our affairs. And now, if you will not run away to the English who are coming up the river, but serve our interest, I will acquaint monsieur of it on his return from France, which will be very pleasing to him; and I now give my word you shall have liberty to go to Boston on the first opportunity; if you desire it, or any other favor in my power shall not be denied you."

I replied: "Madam, it is contrary to the nature of the English to requite evil for good. I shall endeavor to serve you and your interest. I shall not run to the English, but if I am taken by them I shall willingly go with them, and yet endeavor not to disserve you, either in your person or goods."

The place where we lived was called Hagimsack, twenty-five leagues from the river's mouth, as I have before stated.

We now embarked and went in a large boat and canoe two or three miles up an eastern branch of the river that comes from a large pond, and on the following evening sent down four hands to make discovery. And while they were sitting in the house the English surrounded it and took one of the four. The other three made their escape in the dark and through the English soldiers, and coming to us, gave a surprising account of affairs. Upon this news madam said to me, "Little English, now you can go from us, but I hope you will remember your word." I said, "Madam, be not concerned. I will not leave you in this strait." She said, "I know not what to do with my two poor little babes." I said, "Madam, the sooner we embark and go over the great pond the better." Accordingly we embarked and went over the pond. The next day we spoke with Indians, who were in a canoe, and they gave us an account that Signecto town was taken and burnt. Soon after we heard the great guns at Gov. Villebon's fort, which the English engaged several days. They killed one man, then drew off down the river, fearing to continue longer for fear of being frozen in for the winter, which in truth they would have been.

Hearing no report of cannon for several days, I, with two others, went down to our house to make discovery. We found our young lad who was taken by the English when they went up the river. The general had shown himself so honorable, that on reading the note on our door, he ordered it not to be burnt, nor the barn. Our cattle and other things he preserved, except one or two, and the poultry for use. At their return they ordered the young lad to be put on shore. Finding things in this posture, we returned and gave madam an account of it.

She acknowledged the many favors which the English had showed her, with gratitude, and treated me with great civility. The next spring monsieur arrived from France in the man of war. He thanked me for my care of his affairs, and said he would endeavor to fulfill what madam had promised me.

Accordingly, in the year 1698, peace being proclaimed, a sloop came to the mouth of the river with ransom for one Michael Cooms. I put monsieur in mind of his word, telling him there was now an opportunity for me to go and see the English. He advised me to continue with him ; said he would do for me as for his own, &c. I thanked him for his kindness, but rather chose to go to Boston, hoping to find some of my relations yet alive. Then he advised me to go up

8

to the fort and take my leave of the governor, which I
did, and he spoke very kindly to me. Some days
after, I took my leave of madam, and monsieur went
down to the mouth of the river with me, to see me
safely on board. He asked the master, Mr. Starkee, a
Scotchman, whether I must pay for my passage, and if
so, he would pay it himself rather than I should have
it to pay at my arrival in Boston, but he gave me not
a penny. The master told him there was nothing to
pay, and that if the owner should make any demand,
he would pay it himself, rather than a poor prisoner
should suffer, for he was glad to see any English person
come out of captivity.

On the 13th of June, I took my leave of monsieur,
and the sloop came to sail for Boston, where we arrived
on the 19th of the same, at night. In the morning
after my arrival, a youth came on board and asked
many questions relating to my captivity, and at length
gave me to understand that he was my little brother
who was at play with some other children at Pemmaquid when I was taken captive, and who escaped into
the fort at that perilous time. He told me my elder
brother, who made his escape from the farm, when it
was taken, and our two little sisters, were alive, but
that our mother had been dead some years. Then we
went on shore and saw our elder brother.

On the 2d of August, 1689, I was taken, and on the
19th of June, 1698, I arrived at Boston, so that I was
absent eight years, ten months, and seventeen days.
In all which time, though I underwent extreme difficulties, yet I saw much of God's goodness. And may

the most powerful and beneficent Being accept of this public testimony of it, and bless my experiences to excite others to confide in his all-sufficiency, through the infinite merits of JESUS CHRIST.

APPENDIX.

CONTAINING MINUTES OF THE EMPLOYMENTS, PUBLIC STATIONS, ETC., OF JOHN GYLES, ESQ., COMMANDER OF THE GARRISON ON ST. GEORGE'S RIVER.

AFTER my return out of captivity, June 28th, 1698, I applied myself to the government for their favor. Soon after, I was employed by old father Mitchel, of Malden, to go as his interpreter on trading account, to St. John's river.

October 14th, 1698, I was employed by the government, Lieutenant Governor Stoughton commander-in-chief, to go as interpreter, at three pounds per month, with Major Converse and old Captain Alden, to Penobscot to fetch captives. At our return to Boston, I was dismissed; but within a few days the governor sent for me to interpret a conference with Bommazeen, and other Indians then in jail.

Some time after, I was again put in pay in order to go interpreter with Col. Phillips and Capt. Southack, in the province galley, to Casco Bay, to exchange said Indians [Bommazeen and others], for English captives. In December, 1698, we returned to Boston with several captives which we had liberated, and I was dismissed the service, and desired to attend it in the spring. I pleaded to be kept in pay that I might have wherewith to support myself at school. I went into the country, to Rowley, where boarding was cheap, to practise what little I had attained at school.

March, 1699. With the little of my wages that I could reserve, I paid for my schooling and board, and attended the service upon request, and was again put into pay, and went with Col. Phillips and Maj. Converse in a large brigantine, up Kennebeck river for captives, and at our return to Boston, the province galley being arrived from New York with my lord Bellemont, and the province truck put on board, I was ordered on board the galley. We cruised on the eastern shore; and in November, 1699, I was put out of pay, though I pleaded to be continued in it, seeing I must attend the service in the spring, and be at considerable expense in the winter for my schooling.

In the spring of 1700, I attended the service, and was under pay again. On August 27th, a fort was ordered to be built at Casco Bay, which was finished on the 6th of October following, and the province truck landed, and I was ordered to reside there as interpreter, with a captain, &c. Not long after, Governor Dudley sent me a lieutenant's commission, with a memorandum on its back, "No further pay but as interpreter, at three pounds per month."

August 10th, 1703. The French and Indians besieged our fort for six days. (Major March was our commander.) On the 16th of the same month, Capt. Southack arrived in the province galley, and in the night following, the enemy withdrew.

May 19th, 1704. I received a few lines from his excellency, directing me to leave my post, and accompany Colonel Church on an expedition round the bay of Fundy.* September following I returned to my post, without any further wages or encouragement for that service than the beforementioned pay at the garrison.

April, 1706. There was a change of the chief officer at our garrison. I chose to be dismissed with my old officer, which was granted. The same year, his excellency, Governor Dudley, presented me with a captain's commission, and ordered Colonel Saltonstall to detach fifty effective men to be delivered to me in order for a march.

In May, 1707, I entered on an expedition under Colonel March, for Port Royal, at the termination of which I was dismissed.

May 12th, 1708, I received orders from his excellency to go to Port Royal with a flag of truce to exchange prisoners, and brought off all. At my return I was dismissed the service.

In 1709, I received a commission, and Colonel Noyes had orders to detach forty men, whom he put under me, with orders to join the forces for Canada. At Hull, August 1st, 1709, I received orders from his excellency to leave my company with my lieutenants, and go to Port Royal with a flag of truce to exchange prisoners. I went in the sloop Hannah and Ruth, Thomas Waters,

* A full account of this expedition under Colonel Church, will be found in Church's History of King Phillip's War, &c., ed. 12mo., Boston, 1827, by S. G. DRAKE.

master. I had nine French prisoners, which were all that were in our governor's hands. These he ordered me to deliver to Governor Supercass, "and to let him know that he [Colonel Dudley] expected him to deliver all the English prisoners within his power, within six days, which I was ordered to demand and insist upon, agreeably to his promise last year." I was ordered to observe to him that Governor Dudley highly resent:d his breach of promise in not sending them early this spring, according to his parole of honor, by myself, when we had returned him upwards of forty of his people, and had made provision for bringing home ours; and to make particular inquiry after Captain Myles, and to demand his and his company's release also.

Accordingly, arriving at Port Royal, I was kindly entertained by Governor Supercass; brought off one hundred prisoners. Soon after my return our forces were dismissed, and I received no other consideration for my services than pay as captain of my company.

August, 1715. I was desired, and had great promises made me by the proprietors, and received orders from his excellency, to build a fort at Pejepscot [now Brunswick, Me]. Soon after our arrival there the Indians came in the night, and forbid our laying one stone upon another. I told them I came with orders from Governor Dudley to build a fort, and if they disliked it, they might acquaint him with it; and that if they came forcibly upon us, they or I should fall on the spot. After such like hot words they left us, and we went on with our building, and finished it November 25th, 1715, and our carpenters and masons left us.

My wages were very small, yet the gentlemen proprietors ordered me only five pounds for my good services, &c.

July 12th, 1722, a number of Indians engaged fort George about two hours, killing one person, and then drew off to killing cattle, &c.

April, 1725, I received orders from his honor, Lieut. Governor Dummer, to go ten days' march up Ammiscoggin river, and in my absence the Indians killed two men at our fort. I received no further pay for said service, only the pay of the garrison.

December 12th, 1725, I was dismissed from fort George, and Capt. Woodside received a commission for the command of that place.

December 13th, 1725, I was commissioned for the garrison at St. George's river.

September, 1726. I was detained some months from my post by order of Governor Dummer, to interpret for the Cape Sable Indians, who were brought in and found guilty.* There was no other person in the province that had their language. His honor, and the honorable council, presented me with ten pounds for this service, which I gratefully received.

November 28th, 1728, I was commissioned for the peace.

I have had the honor to serve this province under eight commanders-in-chief, governors, and lieutenant

---

* There were five of them belonging to the St. Francis tribe. They had seized on a vessel at New Foundland, belonging to Plymouth. The act being considered piracy, they were all executed at Boston.—S. G. DRAKE. (MS. Chronicles of the Indians.)

governors, from the year 1698 to the year 1736; and how much longer my services may continue, I submit to the Governor of the world, who overrules every circumstance of life, which relates to our happiness and usefulness, as in infinite wisdom he sees meet.